The Wild and Crazy Adventures

of a

Boy Named Will

William Boswell

Illustrations by Michelle Matson

ISBN: 1453653406
ISBN-13: 9781453653401

My first book is dedicated
to Mimi, my grandmother.
She is a good listener
and the fastest speller.

The Pig That Did Not Go To Market

This is a story about an orphaned pig. It is about a pig that did *not* go to market. Here is how it happened. My good friend Aiden and I were so busy fighting off pirates and fire breathing dragons from his tree house that day, I forgot about going home until it was almost dark. When I realized how late it was, I hopped down and ran inside to call Mama. "Can I take the shortcut through the forest, Mama?" I asked, even though I know she doesn't like that. "Just this once," I pleaded.

"Okay," she answered slowly, not very happy with me. "But I'm walking to meet you." She knows I don't like it when she has to walk to meet me, but I didn't complain. You see, she worries about some adventure finding her little boy on the forest path.

I was on my way, hurrying along the path. I was thinking about the evil pirate captain Aiden and I had almost captured that afternoon, but I really *was* hurrying. I was trying to get to the edge of the forest before dark, like Mama had said.

Suddenly, I froze in my tracks. I quietly tiptoed backward a few steps. I knew the sound I had heard was not part of my daydreaming. It was an unusual sound, not something anyone might expect to hear in the forest behind their house in the middle of a city. What I heard was the sound of a pig. Not a big pig sound, just a little bitty pig sound. It seemed to be coming from a pile of brush next to the path. I carefully lifted the dried vines to see if I could see what was making the sound. There, curled up in a ball, was a baby pig no bigger than a loaf of cinnamon bread.

The little pig was sleeping, snoring, and snorting, like a little pig. I listened carefully to see if I could hear any other pig sounds in the forest, but no, it was just the little pig. I thought and thought but could not decide about the right thing to do. I looked at the little pig, all pink and warm, and wondered where its mother could have gone without her baby. Mothers don't just leave their babies sleeping all alone in a forest. Even I know that.

I waited and waited for her to return and take care of her baby, but when the sun was almost hidden behind the trees, I decided I better tuck the little fella into my sweatshirt and bring it on home with me for two important reasons. Number one, my mother would be really unhappy if she saw me stopped in the forest, and number two, I didn't think little piggy would be safe in the forest alone all night. I tucked him in and hurried along. I was thinking about what my mother was going to say. I was also wondering if the pig's parents had been taken away to the zoo by a hunter who didn't know there was a baby pig to be taken care of.

When I saw my mom on the path, she stopped and put her hands on her hips like she does if she's been waiting for me and she thinks I've been dawdling, but I hadn't. I started to tell her right away. Before I could say a word, she said to me, "Now, Will, please. Don't tell me a giant hawk swooped down and pulled you backward by the seat of your pants and you had to hold tight onto a tree until he stopped pulling, and that's what kept you." It sounded like an adventure I may have had before. But just about then, she stopped talking and took a breath, and in the quietness, she heard the sound of a little pig snoring and snorting.

It sounded like *sngggg, snk, snk, snk.* "What is that noise coming from you?" she asked, still with her hands on her hips. I reached around and lifted little piggy from the hood of my sweatshirt. I held him out to show Mama and told her the story.

My mother is very kind. She agreed that the baby pig needed to be rescued. She said I could keep him for one night, "and one night only," until I could find someplace suitable for a pig to live.

When we got back to our house on Ohio Street and everyone had gotten settled in for the night, I decided that the pig was so little and sweet, he would be more comfortable and less lonely if I quietly carried him up to my bedroom and kept him there, just for the night. I put my fuzzy Batman pajamas in the bottom of a box the new microwave had come in and then I gently laid little piggy down. Everything seemed fine.

In the middle of the night, though, when it was very dark and quiet in the house, tiny piggy grunting and snorting sounds woke me up. The *snort snort snort* was coming from the box next to my bed. The little piggy was stretching up on his back legs with his front feet reaching almost to my pillow. Two little pink piggy eyes were looking up at me, and his little pink nose was reaching closer to me with each tiny snort.

It seemed to me that little piggy was trying to tell me something. I did not want Mama and Daddy to hear what he had to say. I picked him up and rubbed his smooth, pink little belly a bit, trying to soothe him, but little piggy kept on snorting. Quietly, I tiptoed downstairs so we could figure it out without waking my family. The little pig slurped some water from my dog Clyde's bowl. He licked his lips after the little bit of leftover spaghetti I gave him—and the meatball, wow! It really disappeared fast.

But he still made little piggy noises, and it seemed that he wanted something else. I decided to take him outside and see if he needed to go pee pee or poo poo. Fortunately, that's exactly what little piggy had been trying to say. I really think he smiled when he nuzzled my face just a bit as I picked him up to help him back inside. He seemed happy that I understood pig snort.

When we went back to bed, little piggy bounced around and around in the box. He used his back legs for climbing, and pretty soon he stood on the edge of the box. Then he climbed up and onto my bed. He plunked down on half of my only pillow. I let him do

it. I remember thinking, *What could it hurt?* The piggy wasn't hungry, he wasn't thirsty, he probably wouldn't need to go potty for a while, and he was a very tiny little piggy who didn't know where his mother was. He was probably feeling a little bit like an orphan.

I was tired and so I went back to sleep, but then I heard the *snort snort* noise again. "Oh no," I moaned. "This is turning into a nightmare!" I thought the little piggy wanted something else, but I realized, no, the little snorter was fast asleep, curled up on the pillow right next to my ear. The snorting only sounded so loud because it was so close. I listened for a while until I got used to the noise and then I began to think, *Hmm, this isn't so terrible.* It was a little bit like listening to big fat rain drops bumping into your window on a dark night.

Weeks and then months went by while me and Mama tried to find a place suitable for a sweet little pig to live, we really did. It was not that easy. We thought about a farm; we thought about a zoo. Daddy said that if little piggy kept growing like he was, we should think about the market.

It was true: little piggy was getting big. He had grown big enough that my little brother, Wyatt, could go for rides around the house on his back. They both had fun,

except when little piggy decided to run up the stairs. Little piggy had very smooth skin, you see. Sometimes that made it hard for Wyatt to hold on, and little piggy would squeal like crazy.

Mama was happy because little piggy always let someone know when he had to go to the bathroom. All they had to do was open the door for him. We didn't even have to wipe his butt. It was like magic how clean he stayed. I don't know why pigs have such a reputation of being, well, you know, piggy.

Daddy was happy because he and Mama never had to use the garbage disposal anymore. Little piggy cleaned up all the leftovers.

Little piggy enjoyed a happy life at our house, spending his days playing with me and Wyatt and the neighborhood boys in the backyard. He could play hide-and-seek, and he never peeked until we were ready. He even learned to climb the ladder and could get up into my tree house, although we sometimes thought he would crash for certain, and it never looked easy.

After a while, he became too big to climb the ladder because Daddy was afraid he would break it. Then little piggy discovered he could get up to the tree house by using the slide. That worked just great. There was only

one thing about the tree house we never could convince him to try and that was the zip line. That's where he drew the line. He said, "No deal." I tried to get Daddy to make him a special harness for the zip line, but that's where Daddy drew the line. He also said, "No deal."

More time passed, and little piggy grew and grew until one night, I woke up from a sound sleep feeling hot, sweaty, and uncomfortable. I had so little room for me in my bed, and my bed sagged in the middle. I thought for a minute about how I weighed forty pounds and how little piggy had grown to two hundred and forty pounds.

I decided right then what I had to do. It was time for little piggy to move into his own bed.

The next morning, I took him out to the backyard and explained my plan. "Little pig," I said, "I don't have any room in my bed for me anymore. We're going to have to find you a new place to sleep. You need to begin staying in the backyard." Well, little piggy began to whimper and snort, but I listened carefully and then said, "Wait a minute, wait a minute. You're not going to market, no, no, no. You are *not* going to market! Daddy was only teasing. You will still be part of our family. You can still come to our birthday parties and always have

the leftover cake and ice cream. Daddy and I will build you a house that looks a little like a dog house but it will be a little piggy house. When my friends are over for a play date, we'll come outside and you can still show them all of your kung fu moves. But you've gotten to be a very big and strong little pig, and you just can't try slicing any more trees in half. You know how that upsets Daddy."

Daddy the Snake Fighter

There was a weird noise in the backyard. We could hear it from inside our house. Me, Daddy, and my little brother, Wyatt, all heard it. When we looked outside, we were shocked. I started yelling because I was so shocked. Wyatt yelled, "Daddy, Daddy, go help the froggie, Daddy. Go quick!" he said as he grabbed Daddy's pant leg and pulled him toward the patio door.

I could see Daddy was thinking so I said, "Go, Daddy, go make a rescue. You know you can do it!" I said that mostly because that's what Daddy would have said to me.

Daddy looked out the window a second longer, scratching his chin. Then he said, "Meet me on the back porch, boys. I've got to get something out of the garage."

When Daddy came out of the garage, he was pulling on his gardening gloves, or as me and Wyatt called them that day, his snake-fighting gloves.

For some strange reason, which I still don't understand, one of the garter snakes that live in our backyard had clamped his mouth down on a big frog. The frog was crying and kicking, but he couldn't get away.

I asked Daddy why he needed the gloves, and he said, "Well, son, what if Mr. Snake doesn't want to give up the frog? I don't want to have to squeal like a little girl. Come on," he said, "let's go make a rescue."

Daddy grabbed that snake just behind his head and he held him up in the air to look him in the eye. The poor frog was really crying loud, so me and Wyatt started yelling as loud as we could. "Hey, Mr. Snake," we yelled, "you let that frog go!"

Daddy said, "Will, go inside and get the video camera. Mama is not going to believe this!" I ran inside but Wyatt continued the yelling by himself.

Just then, the lady from next door and her big poodle came running over and she asked Daddy, "What's wrong, what's wrong? Is everything all right? Why are the boys so upset?"

Daddy was busy so he didn't hear her at first with the frog crying like I've never heard a frog cry before, and Wyatt yelling, and me calling out from inside the house that I had found the video camera. So she came closer and asked Daddy again, "What's wrong, what's wrong?"

When you get to know Daddy, you will see he has a way of looking at you when he is asking you to explain yourself, and he doesn't have to say a word. He just raises those big eyebrows of his and you know. Well, our neighbor didn't understand the raised eyebrows like we do, because she came closer to Daddy and she asked him again, "What is the yelling all about, for goodness sakes?" But then she saw the snake with his mouth clamped down on the frog. It was a huge frog, like a bull frog. That silly snake. It was impossible for him to ever swallow such a big frog. The neighbor started yelling, too.

It was crazy in our backyard by the time I got there with the video camera. Daddy had to ask the neighbor lady to calm down. We were trying to document this very unusual event. He explained to her that he didn't want the only sound to be a bunch of people yelling.

She closed her mouth and just watched as I held the video camera steady and told Daddy, "I'm ready, Daddy." He grabbed that snake's mouth with his other hand and pried its jaws open.

As soon as the big old frog dropped to the ground, the snake was not happy. He whipped around furiously and flipped himself right out of Daddy's hands. The neighbor lady suddenly didn't care about all the yelling anymore. She took off running as fast as she could. All we heard from her was her back door slamming. Daddy grabbed the frog in one hand and Wyatt in the other. He said, "Inside, Will."

We put the frog in the kitchen sink and washed him up. He seemed to be doing okay after a while so we delivered him to my favorite spot in our yard, the vegetable garden. We haven't seen the angry snake again, and I hope we don't.

Blue Gill Fishing: Not Your Ordinary Day

It was show-and-tell day at school. I knew we had to go to the lake to set my tadpole free. That is what got me thinking. When Daddy came to pick me up from pre-school, I told him what I had been thinking about all morning. I was thinking about Blue Gill fishing. Daddy signed me out and said, "Good-bye, Ms. Monica. We're off to free a future frog."

I asked if we could fish while we were at the lake, and Daddy said, "Sure, Will." So far, it seemed like an ordinary day, until I cast my line into the water.

Daddy always says, "If you want to catch a little fish you must use little bait. If you want to catch a big fish, use big bait." He tells me so much though. Sometimes I forget something important. That's what happened.

I didn't feel like putting a little squiggly worm on my hook. I reached into the tackle box and found a good-sized lure. I tied it on and cast out quickly before Daddy could say, "Stop and think, Will." The very first bite of the day was a big surprise.

I didn't know fish that big lived in the little lake by our house. This fish didn't wait for the bait to come to him. No, sir! I saw him leap up out of the water and grab my bait. It seemed like he wanted to be caught. I tried to set the hook like Daddy taught me so I could start to reel him in. Instead, that fish reeled me out. He lifted me right out of my fishing boots and left them sitting on the bank. I wondered if he was trying to use me for bait. That big fish dragged me completely around the lake once. We were moving so fast, maybe it was twice. Daddy was on the shore, waving his arms and yelling, "Hey, you monster fish, bring my boy back here!" I could hear him, and he wasn't happy.

Here's what happened. I held on tight to my reel as we raced around and around the lake. Every time I got a chance, I reeled in my line a little bit more, a little bit more. After a lot of work, I got up close enough to get a really good look at the fish that had yanked me into the water.

He was a big one, all right, and he seemed to be having fun. He kept looking back to make sure I was still there. I kept reeling. I reeled and I reeled and I reeled. Then, I got close enough that I could hop up on his back. I grabbed him by the fins and held on tight. I used those fins and steered us back to shore.

He took me back to shore just as fast as he had taken me away. I slid off over his nose and landed right next to my fishing boots. I got a good look at that big fish for a minute. He had a gleam in his eye. He seemed friendly. I really don't think he meant any harm. I think he only wanted to have some fun. He just didn't understand how seriously Daddy would take having his boy dragged all around the lake once, maybe twice.

Little Bear Breaks A Leg

My whole family met at a park last summer for a big party. We were celebrating my cousin's graduation from high school. We ate hotdogs and hamburgers, cake and ice cream, and a lot of watermelon. I played hide-and-seek with the cousins my age. Then we played on the swings and slides and the merry-go-round until I thought I would throw up. It was time for a new activity. I asked my grandmother, "What's behind the woods in back of the lodge?"

When I heard there was a river running back there, I wanted to go for a walk and maybe throw some rocks in the water. I always like to throw rocks into water. We cleared it with Mama. Daddy was already playing horse shoes with the other men, so I didn't have to ask him. Off we walked.

The river was actually very far and I was beginning to think Mimi, my grandmother, had been mistaken and there really wasn't a river. We were walking along a dirt path with trees on both sides and I couldn't see or hear a river. Some people say they can smell a river; well I couldn't. I was kicking rocks and grumbling. I wanted to get to the river. I had started to think about getting my feet wet. The path took another turn and I didn't hear the river, but suddenly, Mimi stopped and stood very still. She put her hand on my shoulder and slowly tried to pull me behind her.

"What?" I wanted to know, moving back around. It was then I saw what had made her stop in her tracks. A big old bear was sitting down right in the path. He had his head down, and if you've never seen a bear cry, I'll tell you it was a very sad thing to see. Those big shoulders were shaking, and he wasn't just crying, he was sobbing. Although Mimi tried to *shhhh* me, I couldn't help it. I had to ask, "Mr. Bear, what's the problem?"

The noise stopped for a minute, and the bear looked at me and shook his big old head and then lowered it back down and sobbed some more. Mimi gave me the look that said, "Come on; let's go back the way we came," as she slowly started taking small steps backward and pulling me along.

I had to try once more though. "If you can tell me what the problem is, Mr. Bear," I said, "I'll see if I can do something about it. My dad is back at the lodge and he can fix anything."

The bear looked up at me again and I think he believed me. He said, "It, it's my baby. My baby is hurt."

I had to try and pull Mimi with me because she wasn't letting me getting any closer to the bear without her. We got right up to the sad old bear and I laid my hand on his knee. That's about as high as I could reach. In her most kind voice, Mimi said, "If you want to tell us what happened to your baby, Mr. Bear, we will listen."

Between his sobs, the big bear answered, "He jumped off the rock, the big one by the river, and he hurt his leg. The bone is sticking out. He's crying, and I don't know what to do. I'm trying to think of what I can do. I picked him some berries, but he doesn't want them. I caught him a fish, but he isn't hungry. I don't know what to do. Do you?"

"Mimi is a nurse," I said quickly. "Maybe we should go and have a look at your baby bear. I bet Mimi can help. You know, she *is* my dad's mom."

I saw Mimi roll her eyes, but I saw something else, too. That bear was sobbing a little more quietly. He grunted and rolled around and got up on all fours and started down the path toward the river. We followed him.

It wasn't quite as sunny outside when we finally heard the river. The big old bear stopped near a large pile of rocks, or so I thought it was a pile of rocks. He pulled brush away from a big rock and there was an opening. It was a cave. The bear went inside and then Mimi grabbed me by the arm and yanked me back. "I'll check the baby bear," she said. "You wait right here, young man."

Mimi went in but the big bear came back to the cave entrance and showed me the way in. Mimi was nervous, I could tell. She didn't really like the idea of me being in that cave, but I felt fine being there since I had gotten her into this. And besides, I wanted to see what it looked like to have a broken leg with the bone sticking out.

"It's awfully dark in here, Mr. Bear," Mimi said, "can you bring your baby over by the light from outdoors so I can see?" Instead, the big bear went over near where the little bear was lying on the floor of the cave and he began to start a small fire in their fire pit.

Soon the flames were curling up toward the high roof of the cave, and there was plenty of light to see all around. Mimi kneeled down next to the little bear and she said, "Hello, little bear. I'm Mimi, and this is my grandson, Will. Your daddy told us you hurt your leg. We came to see if there is something we can do to help. May I have a look at your leg?" The little bear was trying to be brave, you could tell. He was sniffling, and I could see he had been crying. He was very sad and couldn't move much at all. He turned his head toward us. He reached a little bear paw out and touched Mimi on her knee. He seemed to me to be saying that it was okay for her to look at his leg.

Mimi had a look, and I had a little look, and it was awful. The little bone sticking out was white but there was bear blood all over it and his leg. I just hoped right then that I never had a broken leg with my bone sticking out. I wanted us to do something to help him.

Mimi turned around to the daddy bear and said, "You are right, Mr. Bear. Your baby is really hurt and I'm sorry to say I can't fix it."

Right then I knew it was a crazy idea, but I just couldn't help it. I said, "Well, Mimi, you work at a hospital. Couldn't we take him there and get it fixed?"

The big bear seemed to be thinking, too. Maybe he was praying, I don't know. He had his head bowed, and when he slowly looked up, he said, "Okay, if you can get my baby's leg fixed, I will let you take him to your hospital."

I know Mimi wanted to say it was a hospital for people. I also know that Mimi can be very persuasive when she wants to get something done. I wasn't surprised when she pulled out her cell phone and talked quietly for a moment. Then she said, "Well Mr. Bear, it will be painful when baby bear moves, so I think we are going to have to get a ride to the hospital. If you don't mind, I've called a friend to come and get us." Mr. Bear nodded. He seemed scared and not completely certain this was a good idea, but at least he had stopped that awful sobbing. I think we had given him hope.

We heard the *whop whop whop* of the chopper, and Mimi said to Mr. Bear, "That's our ride. I think we can be back before dark. Are you okay with that?"

"I'll go with you," Mr. Bear promptly said.

Mimi rested her hand on his arm and quietly said, "It's a small helicopter, Mr. Bear. I don't think there is enough room for a grown-up bear."

It was a tough decision for the daddy bear; you could just see it. He carefully picked his baby bear up and placed the little fella in Mimi's arms. "I know you'll take care of him," he said with a sniffle.

I was already outside the cave looking for the chopper because I wanted to see who was driving and where they were going to land. Then, the chopper was right overhead and I realized, they weren't going to land. The side door slid open and a silver basket that looked a little like a bed was lowered down to where we were waiting. Mimi placed baby bear down in the basket. Quickly, she wrapped him up and fastened his safety belt and then tugged on the harness. Baby bear was whisked up to the chopper.

Mimi took my hand and said, "They'll send a harness down for us. I'll hold you tight."

Just then the big bear took me by the hand and said, "I'll take care of your baby while you're taking care of mine."

Uh oh, I thought, *that's a deal breaker.* I knew I had to talk fast if this was going to work out. "It's okay, Mimi," I said. "I'm going to be safe here with the daddy bear." Mimi didn't answer me. She motioned for the big bear to come back into the cave. I don't know what they said to each other, but when they came out, Mimi fastened herself into the harness, tugged the cable, and up she went.

The chopper just sat there. Saying *whop, whop whop.* Then, the door opened again and down came a harness. Daddy bear got himself fastened in and then he held me tight and up we went. Mimi had made room for us.

It was just getting dark by the time the helicopter dropped the bears back off at their cave. Of course, Mimi had to give the daddy bear some instructions about taking care of baby bear's new cast. Giving instructions is something nurses do for all their patients.

It was Mimi's idea to have the chopper drop us off just in back of the lodge, and it was a good thing, too. No sooner had our feet hit the ground and the *whop whop whop* faded away did we see Mama and Daddy and a group of other adults coming with flashlights. Mama had organized a search party. Right after she hugged me, she asked, "Where have you been? I thought you were lost!"

That's not what Daddy thought, though. He looked first at me and then at his mom. He said, "Hmmm. You two have been off on some grand adventure, I'll bet."

Coming Soon in Book # 2

Heroes, Ghosts, and Termites From Mars

William and Isabelle at Sea

The Spooky Tale of the Missing Dogs

Termites From Mars

The Littlest Turtle

The Case of the Visiting Ghost

Illustrator Michelle Matson

Michelle lives in Oak Forest, IL, with her young family. She has been an artist since childhood. This is her first time doing illustrations for a children's book.

6861079R0

Made in the USA
Charleston, SC
17 December 2010